The Quest for Queenie

by Brian Ball

Illustrated by Lisa Thiesing

SPRINGBOARD
B·O·O·K·S

Little, Brown and Company

Boston   Toronto   London

BAL

Once more, for Maureen

Text copyright © 1988 by Brian Ball
Illustrations copyright © 1991 by Lisa Thiesing

First U.S. Edition
First published in Great Britain in 1988 by Simon & Schuster Young Books

Library of Congress Cataloging-in-Publication Data

Ball, Brian, 1932–
   The quest for queenie / by Brian Ball; illustrated by Lisa Thiesing. — 1st
U.S. ed.
     p.   cm.
   Summary: Harry and Jill are chosen by a magic talking sword to rescue a
damsel from the Bad Wizard of Mandragora, but the damsel is Harry's com-
placent, fat spaniel, who decides she doesn't want to be rescued after all.
   ISBN 0-316-07961-8 (reinforced)
   [1. Fantasy.]   I. Thiesing, Lisa, ill.   II. Title.
PZ7.B1983Qu   1991
[E] — dc20   90-45687

Springboard Books and design is a registered trademark of
Little, Brown and Company (Inc.)

10 9 8 7 6 5 4 3 2 1

WOR
PRINTED IN THE UNITED STATES OF AMERICA

The Quest
for Queenie

1

Harry was kicking a Coke can along the gutter, and his cousin Jill was blowing a huge pink bubble-gum bubble. They were on their way home from school together, and as usual they were arguing.

This time, they were quarreling about the old legends they had read in Ms. Panko's class all week.

"Princes and swords and ogres are best," said Harry, as he booted the Coke can.

Jill popped the big pink bubble. "Stupid," she told Harry. "The one about the damsel and the dragon was best."

"It was corny," said Harry. "The one-eyed ogre was better. You know, when he ate up the prince and the others who'd gone rescuing. He ate the arms and legs and everything. I liked him. I bet I wouldn't be scared of him."

"You!" said Jill scornfully. "You hide behind the couch when there's a scary movie on TV. Not scared of an ogre — sure!"

Harry didn't try to hit her. Jill did tae kwon do, and she was learning to break bricks with her bare hands. He wasn't going to take any chances with her. So he booted the Coke can high up onto the rubble and dust and bricks, where the old supermarket had been knocked down by bulldozers last week.

Harry ran up onto the rubble to kick the can down again.

Then he saw something glittering in the rubble. It wasn't the Coke can. It was shining like a million rainbows.

"Come on down, Harry!" ordered Jill. "We've got to meet Queenie."

Queenie was Harry's old spaniel. She spent most of her time dreaming that she was a puppy again. When she dreamed, her legs went fast and her nose twitched faster. She was running runs and smelling smells from when she was young. When school was over, she woke up. Then she scratched herself and went to meet Harry and Jill.

"Harry, come on! Queenie!" Jill called impatiently.

But Harry wasn't thinking about Queenie. And he didn't hear Jill's shouts.

He was rubbing his eyes, dazzled by this whatever-it-was flashing and glittering in the rubble. Harry's fingers and toes tingled, and little electric shocks prickled the back of his neck. He blinked and looked down at the weird lights.

What was it?

There were diamonds and rubies and sapphires and emeralds, and gold, too, and it was something stuck there in the rubble.

Harry felt faint. His knees went wobbly, and his ears felt frozen like fish sticks.

"Harry, what are you doing up there?" called Jill.

Since he wouldn't answer her, she climbed up to join him.

"Look," whispered Harry. "I found something. It has a handle, with jewels on it and things. I think it's a sword!"

Jill was going to tell him not to be his usual stupid self, but then she saw the marvelous rainbows flashing in the dust and rubble of the old supermarket. And she felt odd and tingly, too.

"I only came to kick the can down, and just look what I found," said Harry.

"Don't touch it, Harry," Jill said, because it looked so *weird,* but she was too late. "Harry!"

Harry had already pulled hard on the glittering

handle, and out came the sword, bright and sharp, long and broad. Finding that it wasn't as heavy as it looked, he waved it around his head, and Jill was just going to tell him to watch it, he might chop someone's head off if he wasn't careful, when a deep voice boomed out, "Hail, O Harry! Hail, Harry the Hero!"

Harry leaped about two feet into the air, closely followed by Jill.

When they landed in the bricks and dust again, they looked at each other fearfully.

Harry whispered, "Who said that?"

"I don't know," Jill murmured back, though she did know. "Do you think it was the sword, Harry?"

Harry looked at the long steel blade. "No," he squeaked. "No. It couldn't have been."

"It was!" thundered the deep voice. "It was I, Sigismund, the Magical Sword of Mandragora!"

Harry looked at the blade, then at the handle. And then he tried to let go of this odd, shouting whatever-it-said-it-was. He lifted it up and swung it around a couple of times and tried to chuck it as far as he could. The trouble was that when he opened his hand and let it go, it *didn't* go. And it *wouldn't* go.

"Magic?" said Jill faintly. "Throw it away, Harry!"

"I tried to!" Harry wailed. "It won't let me, Jill. It's stuck in my hand."

"That's right," declared the sword. "We're stuck with each other now, O Harry." And as Jill made a dismal-sounding *ploppp* with her pink bubble, the sword went on, "I'm sorry, but once the magic's started, there's no stopping it."

"What?" Harry cried, feeling quite bewildered.

"Harry means what magic do you mean?" said Jill, and she added, "Please?" so it sounded more polite.

Harry tried again to let go of this glittering talking sword-thing, but it boomed out that it was no use trying.

"We are now inseparable," it said. "And the magic I mean is the kind of magic you two were talking about just now."

"What, when we were talking about those old stories? The ones we read in Ms. Panko's class this week?" Jill asked.

"Exactly!" answered Sigismund. "The old magic lives on for those who believe in it, and you two are believers. You, O damsel, and you more than anyone, O noble Harry! I've been looking around for a likely lad for a few centuries now, since there are none left on Mandragora, and when I heard your brave and bold words, I knew that I had found my hero at last."

"Me?" said Harry.

"Him?" said Jill. "My cousin Harry with the carroty hair and stick-out ears and knobby knees?" Then she remembered how Harry had boasted about not being scared of the ogre, and it began to make some sense.

She liked being called O damsel, so she

thought she had better listen to what this weird but impressive sword had to say.

Harry was getting over his first fright, too. He liked being called a hero. It was time he had some excitement in his life. And there wasn't much on TV today.

"So we're sort of stuck with each other, right, er . . . er . . . Sigismund?"

"Indeed we are, O Harry," replied the sword. "Together we shall undergo terrible hazards and do heroic deeds in our desperate quest. Oh, and by the way, you can call me Siggy. Sigismund is a bit long."

"All right," said Harry. "And you can stop saying O Harry, and just call me Harry, if you like, Siggy."

But Siggy said no, it was traditional for a hero to be "O hero" or, in Harry's case, "O Harry," so Harry said all right, fine.

He twirled Siggy around his head and made a few million rainbows over the rubble, and he could just see himself doing heroic deeds. Jill was thinking about doing deeds and things, too.

If Harry was going on a desperate quest, then he wasn't going without *her!* Jill wasn't going to be left out. No way.

2

"So what sort of desperate quest will it be?" Jill asked Siggy.

"Our desperate quest?" said Siggy. "It will be fearful and dangerous." He boomed out the words, and the children knew he was thoroughly enjoying himself. "There will be impossible tasks to be performed. Three of them, as is traditional. There will be an enchanted forest, with wicked trees! And a dragon waiting to breathe fire and smoke. And in the forest, there will be a clearing, and in the midst of the clearing there will be a one-eyed ogre waiting to tear and bite and grind and swallow anyone who might approach!"

Harry gulped as he listened. An *ogre? That ate people?*

"Did you say there will be an ogre?" he managed to ask.

"Waiting to meet you in combat!" answered Siggy, with a happy laugh. "You'll like meeting him, Harry."

"I will?" Harry gulped. "Are you sure?"

Jill didn't pay any attention to Harry's doubts. She had important questions to ask. Before Siggy could start booming any more about ogres, she said, "Well, how does it get started, this desperate quest?"

"How does it get started, O damsel?" He laughed. "I told you. It's already started."

Harry looked around the bricks and dust fearfully.

"It has?" he said.

"Yes!" exclaimed Siggy. "The Bad Wizard gets

things going as soon as I find my hero. By now he'll be plotting something wicked and evil for you, Harry."

This was the first time that either Jill or Harry had heard about a bad wizard, but *that* made sense, too. There were lots of bad wizards in the old legends.

"What sort of things will he be doing?" asked Jill.

Siggy told them. The traditional way of doing it was this: the bad wizard went to the hero's palace and stole the beautiful damsel.

"I expect he's already been to your palace and taken the beautiful damsel, Harry."

"My *what?*" said Harry. "But I haven't got a palace — we live in Belle Vue Mansions. And there *aren't* any beautiful damsels in our house — there's only my mom." Harry was feeling quite relieved by now. He wouldn't have to meet any ogres, after all. "And my mom won't be back from work yet," he finished.

Siggy pondered for a moment.

"Moms don't count," he said finally. "Don't you know *any* beautiful damsels?"

Jill suddenly felt a shock of delight. She had braces, and she was covered in freckles, but she knew that one day she would grow up and be beautiful, and she really wasn't bad-looking now.

So she blushed a bit and said modestly, "Well, there's me, Siggy, isn't there? I'm a beautiful damsel."

"You!" bawled her cousin. "*You!* Skinny Jill, with those braces and — "

He started hooting with laughter. It was the kind of hooting that only unpleasant and insensitive boys can make, boys who have no respect for a girl's private feelings.

So Jill gave him a sharp chop with the edge of her hand, and if Siggy hadn't been a magic sword he'd have gone flying out of Harry's grasp. Siggy sighed.

"Stop squabbling, you two," he said. "You,

O Jill, are in no danger from the Bad Wizard. He wouldn't dare to try to capture you when Harry the Hero is here to guard you from hazards."

"Guard me!" Jill grumbled. "This wimp?"

Harry started to argue, but Siggy stopped him.

"Could I tell you a bit about the Bad Wizard of Mandragora, Harry?" he said. "Bad wizards are always sneaky and evil and wicked, but the Bad Wizard of Mandragora is the sneakiest bad wizard ever."

"So what's he going to do that's so sneaky and bad?" asked Jill.

Harry gave Siggy another twirl or two.

"You're giving me a headache," snapped Siggy. "Stop whirling me around and let me think." After a pause, he exclaimed, "I know, Harry! The Bad Wizard cannot capture your beautiful damsel, so he will steal your favorite charger. Harry, by now he will have stolen your horse!"

Jill and Harry looked at each other. What horse?

"Harry doesn't have a horse," Jill told Siggy.

Siggy didn't like that. "No horse, Harry?"

"No," said Harry. "We only have an old spaniel. She should have come to meet us, but we haven't seen her yet, have we, Jill?"

"No," said Jill. "And Queenie wouldn't wake up if half a dozen bad wizards came knocking at the door."

"You have a dog?" said the magic sword to Harry. "A faithful old hound who was ever the companion of your youth? Why, I wouldn't be surprised if the Bad Wizard of Mandragora has stolen your faithful hound!"

"You mean Queenie?" said Harry, who was feeling a bit bolder by now.

"Well," said Siggy, "if there's no beautiful damsel to be stolen, nor a favorite battle charger, then the Bad Wizard must have made off with — what did you call your hound?"

"Queenie," said Harry. He started to laugh. It was crazy to think that anyone would steal old

Queenie. He laughed a bit more, and then he heard more laughing.

"Ho-ho-ho-ho!" it went. "Ha-ho-ha-ho-ha-ho-ho-ho!"

"That wasn't me laughing," said Harry. "Was it?"

So who *was* laughing in that nasty and sneaky sort of way?

"Oh, dear," said Jill, as another lot of sneaky *ho-ha-ho-ho-ho's* went echoing along the heaps of rubble and dust. "You're right, Siggy. It really *has* started."

3

"The Bad Wizard!" cried Jill.

It was, no doubt about it.

He came in a banging and fizzing of green flashes and yellow smoke.

Fizzzzz! And he was there.

He had a tall black wizard's hat with stars and moons and things, a rusty black cloak that nearly covered his long, rusty legs, and he had long black shoes that curled back to his rusty ankles. He had a wizard's face, a wizard's bony hands, and everything else a particularly wicked wizard traditionally had: a long, bony nose, long, thin ears, and evil eyes.

Harry jumped back, and Jill did, too, but they didn't have time to say excuse me or to argue, for the Bad Wizard was already saying the usual bad things.

But Harry didn't listen to the Bad Wizard. He could hear something else. And it sounded just like Queenie. It sounded just as if Queenie had woken up from one of her dreams and was barking to him.

"Wowwww-wowwwww!" Queenie seemed to be saying. *"Wowww-uuu-wowwww?"*

Jill, though, was listening to the Bad Wizard of Mandragora's wicked words. They were spiteful and evil words.

"Here again, are you, Sigismund the Sorry?" cackled the Bad Wizard. "Have you found another silly little hero for me? Don't bother to answer! I know you have. Just tell him I've captured his slobbery old spaniel, and if he wants to get her back, he'll have to come to Mandragora

to get her! Ho-ho-ha-ha-ho-ho-ho-ho-ha! And there'll be three completely impossible tasks waiting for him when he comes! If he dares!"

There was another series of flashes and bangs, and then the Wizard was gone, but not before he called, "I'm going to give your sorry old spaniel to my friend, the dragon of Mandragora! Byeeeeeee!"

Harry groaned. Wasn't that Queenie he had heard barking?

But where was she barking *from?* It sounded as though she were just a few yards away, but he hadn't seen a twitch of her tail or a lick of her tongue.

"Queenie?" called Harry. "Siggy, I just heard her. Where is she?"

"O Harry, you must know that bad wizards are sneaky and evil!" bellowed the magic sword. "And they have invisibility sacks. Your faithful hound was taken away in just such a magic sack, O Harry. You could not see it, and now she is gone. Gone to Mandragora!"

"You mean, the Bad Wizard's got her?" said Harry.

"Of course he has," said Jill. "What did you think he was doing?"

But Harry wasn't listening. "Taken my Queenie?" he growled. "The Bad Wizard can't do that!"

Siggy liked the sound of Harry now.

"Getting angry, are we, O Harry? Good!"

"Did you say he's taken our Queenie?" Harry was yelling.

He whirled Siggy around his head dangerously, so that the magic sword whistled and laughed.

"I like my heroes angry," Siggy said to Jill. "Just listen to Harry getting mad about the Bad Wizard! I told you he'd be a real hero."

Jill was delighted by it all. It was much more exciting than TV and stories.

"Come on, Harry!" urged the magic sword. "How about yelling with rage and making a few threats to the Bad Wizard?"

Harry didn't need much encouraging. He was whizzing Siggy around his head and jumping up and down with rage.

"If I *dare?*" he yelled. "Well, I dare all right. Just wait till I catch up with that Bad Wizard. I'll make mincemeat out of him! I'll — "

"Harry, stop!" Jill called sharply, so Harry did. "Just shut up a minute," she told him.

"Why?" asked Harry.

"Harry, that's our quest!" she exclaimed. "The Bad Wizard's stolen Queenie, and to get her back we have to go to Mandragora. Poor Queenie is going to be held captive by the dragon, and that's where we'll find her."

Harry stopped whirling the magic sword around his head. He sat down on a chunk of concrete for a moment.

Mandragora? Well, he'd better get there quick. Jill was right.

But what was that she'd said?

Hadn't she said, "That's *our* quest"?

"Hold on, Jill," said Harry. "I'm going to

Mandragora. Siggy's going to Mandragora. But who said anything about *you* going to Mandragora?"

Jill popped the large pink bubble-gum bubble she was blowing.

"Huh," she said. "You're not going anywhere without me, O Harry!"

4

First, they went back to Belle Vue Mansions, just in case it was all a mistake. Maybe it wasn't Queenie in the invisibility sack after all.

But both Harry and Jill knew that it was.

Siggy grumbled about what a waste of time it was. He'd been waiting for hundreds of years, and what was happening now?

"Hasten, O Harry!" he grunted.

"I am!" snapped Harry, turning the key in the lock. "Was it really Queenie in the invisibility sack, Siggy?"

Siggy gave an irritated moan and said of course it was. Bad wizards like the Bad Wizard of Mandragora delighted in tricks like that.

"Poor Queenie!" Jill said.

She looked behind the couch and in the cellar. Harry looked in his bedroom (and especially under the bed). They looked behind the vacuum cleaner in the broom closet. But did they find Queenie? *No.*

"Told you," grumbled Siggy. "The Bad Wizard of Mandragora has her."

"Poor old Queenie," said Harry, but Jill told him he'd better stop moaning and do something.

"You're supposed to be a hero. Get busy being heroic, will you? Queenie's in an invisibility sack, and she's about to become a captive of a dreadful dragon. What must poor Queenie be *thinking!*"

(Actually, Queenie wasn't thinking at all. She was snoring, and dreaming, too. It wasn't a puppy dream; it was a dream about going on a trip and making new friends. Wouldn't it be lovely, she

29

dreamed, to meet a nice friend called the dragon, or something like that, on this wonderful trip to a place called Mandragora? Anyway, that was where the kind man in the black hat and cloak had told her they were going. How delightful, said Queenie to herself in her dream. I've never met a dragon before. The gentleman in the black cloak said that the dragon was longing to meet her. How charming, said Queenie. And she snored some more.)

Harry growled a bit about the Bad Wizard, and Siggy said he was quite right to be angry.

"I told you," said Siggy. "So — it looks like you and I are off to Mandragora."

"And me!" said Jill firmly. "If I can't come, I'll tell your mom where you're going. And I'll tell my mom, too. Then you can't go, can you?"

Harry knew his cousin was right. If Jill said one word about Siggy and Mandragora and dragons and ogres and things like that, then his mom would say he'd been daydreaming, and she'd say go and clean out the bird cage or something just as disgusting.

So Harry grunted, "All right." If Jill was set on coming with him and Siggy, then she'd come.

Harry explained the situation to the magic sword: "Jill has to come, too. To Mandragora."

"Hmmmm," said Siggy. "I suppose she could, if she were a traditional damsel — "

"I am!" Jill declared. "And where he goes, I go!"

There was a noise at the front door just as she said it, and the children jumped, for it was Harry's mom.

"Oh, my poor feet!" she called, and then she bumped down onto the couch.

Harry's mom kicked off her high-heeled shoes. Then she asked where Queenie was and why Harry hadn't put the water on for coffee.

"Queenie?" groaned Harry, trying to hide Siggy behind his back.

"Coffee?" squeaked Jill.

"Yes," said Harry's mom. "I'd love a cup, Jill.

And where's our Queenie, Harry? And what on earth is that thing you're trying to hide behind your back?"

Harry pushed Siggy down behind the chair where Queenie slept, but he couldn't really hide the magic sword. There were too many rubies and diamonds and emeralds and sapphires flashing around. "Oh, goodness me," said Harry's mom, as she saw the Magical Sword of Mandragora. "I suppose you've been wasting your allowance again, Harry. What is it, some more plastic junk?"

Harry looked down at Siggy. What could he say?

Nothing!

But Harry's mom didn't wait for an answer, because just then Jill came in with the coffee. "Oh, that's better," she said. "Now then, Harry, what were you saying about Queenie?"

"Me?" said Harry. Then Siggy hissed that he wasn't to say anything about Queenie going to

Mandragora. Grown-ups weren't supposed to know such things.

"Er . . . er . . . er, Mom — "

He didn't know what to tell her.

"Has Queenie strayed off somewhere?" asked his mom. "Haven't you been looking after that poor old spaniel, Harry?"

"Yes! I mean . . . er . . . "

"Find Queenie!" ordered Harry's mom. "And be back for supper, all of you!"

"I'll see that we get her back," Jill said to Harry's mom. "Come on, Harry."

Jill hurried her cousin out of the house and onto the sidewalk before he could start telling things that grown-ups weren't supposed to know about, like bad wizards and ogres and dragons.

They hadn't gone more than a few steps, though, when Siggy took over.

He started chanting words that sounded like iron bars clanging together. It was scary, but exciting. And it certainly worked, for in a couple of seconds Jill and Harry found themselves whizzing away from Belle Vue Mansions at a tremendous rate.

"It's started," gasped Jill. "We're on our way to Mandragora!"

5

It was like being on a black bus with no lights. Things flashed past them, but they couldn't see what they were.

Once, Jill and Harry saw a star zooming toward them, but it flashed away just as they thought they could feel it crackling and burning. Then they were toppling over and over as if they were on some sort of amusement park ride in space.

"*Yurkkk!*" Harry grunted. "Siggy, when do we get there?"

"Even now, O Harry!" boomed the magic sword. "Behold — Mandragora!"

And suddenly they were *there*.

They were standing on their own feet, but after all that toppling around they felt a little dizzy. Jill shifted her feet, and then she looked down and saw what she was wearing.

"Look at me!" she cried. "I'm a real damsel."

But Harry was looking around at the thick, gloomy forest Siggy had transported them to. There was hardly any sunlight, just enough for the children to see what they were wearing.

"And look at you, Harry," said his cousin.

"What?" asked Harry, and then he looked down, too.

"Tights?" he wailed in dismay. "I'm in tights! And long boots. What'll they say at school if anyone sees me? I'll never be able to go back there! Did you do this, Siggy?"

"It looks all right," said Jill, who was admiring her damsel's outfit. She had on a long, wispy silver gown, with buckled silver shoes, and when

she put her hand to her hair she could feel that it was bound up in some sort of net. "I wish I had a mirror," she said. "This is gorgeous, Siggy."

"It's ridiculous!" yelled Harry.

"It's customary," explained the magic sword. "You've got to look like a hero now, Harry. Just a moment," he said, pausing to chant some magic words. "You wished for a mirror," he said to Jill. "How's that?"

A silver-framed mirror suddenly appeared in Jill's hand, and she was able to see her hair. "I'm gorgeous," she declared, popping a medium-sized bubble of pink bubble gum. "I knew I'd be beautiful in the right clothes. And you don't look so bad. I like the red cloak and the two H's on your chest. Harry the Hero: my cousin. I'm quite proud of you, Harry Taggart. Wowww! What was that?"

She let out a screech as an evil whisper came from above them.

"Going through the Enchanted Forest?" cackled a nasty tree. "Past the ogre? Well, take care, won't you? You know what ogres eat!"

Harry's back and his neck, then his feet, turned cold.

"I'm going back," he said. "I'm giving up being a hero."

"You can't," said Siggy. "Not till you've completed the three tasks and accomplished your quest. You can't return without Queenie."

"Think what your mom would say," said Jill.

"Think what ogres eat!" wailed Harry.

"Yes, I like to think about that," whispered the nasty tree. "Hey, don't do that!" it screeched, as Harry swung Siggy and chopped off a few of its twigs. "I didn't mean it!"

Harry felt better when he heard the nasty tree screech with fright. It made him feel brave again. "I'm not scared," he said, and then a bit louder, "*I'm* not scared. Come on, Jill, let's see what this ogre looks like."

*　*　*

Forward they went along a grim and twisty path, Harry leading with Siggy over his shoulder, and Jill following, making nervous little *plops* with her bubble gum until they came to a clearing.

"Oh, help," groaned Harry. "The ogre!"

And there he was. Huge and one-eyed, with a club in his big hands, grinning at them.

"You know what to do, O Harry," said Siggy briskly.

"Run?" said Harry.

"Yes," squeaked Jill, but Siggy said it was time for Harry to be a hero and fight.

"What?" said Harry. "Fight *that?* All of it? Anyway," he said, looking at the huge mass of the ogre, "what happens if I don't win?"

Siggy got impatient. "Heroes fight; then they win," he said. "Get on with it!"

"Always?" said Harry. "I mean, do they always win?"

Siggy was reluctant to answer. "Well, not quite always," he admitted, at which Harry gave a long and unhappy groan. "But nearly."

"Nearly?" Harry moaned. "Nearly always? But suppose it's me that's one of the *nearlys* and not one of the *alwayses*? Then what, Siggy?"

Siggy didn't answer.

"S-s-siggy?" stuttered Jill. "Come *on!*"

But the magic sword had nothing to say, and the ogre was getting impatient. He rolled his huge club in his hands, and he blinked his awful red eye. "Why are the heroes and the damsels getting smaller and skinnier?" he grumbled. "Two little ones like you are hardly worth eating."

"No, we're not," Jill agreed quickly. She shifted the bubble gum in her mouth so she could be heard better. "Why don't you forget about eating us? You can pretend you haven't seen us, and we'll just creep by. I mean, you can't really like eating people," she finished, but she was so bothered by what she had said that she began to blow a large pink bubble.

"*Like* eating people?" The ogre pondered. "I can't say that I do."

Harry was too shivery and shuddery to join in the conversation. All he could do was watch the ogre, who was watching Jill's bubble-gum bubble as it got larger and larger. It was a wonderful bubble, the largest he had ever seen. The ogre was fascinated, but he hadn't forgotten what he was there for. "No, I don't much like eating people — it's bad for my stomach — but what else can an ogre do? I'm stuck with this job. So, little hero with the magic sword, shall we get on with it?"

But the ogre didn't get on with it. He stared in amazement as the pink bubble stretched and stretched until it hid Jill almost completely.

"What's that?" he demanded.

The bubble couldn't stand the strain anymore. As the ogre took a step forward and Harry took two steps backward, it exploded with a gigantic PLOPPPPPP!

"*Waaauuuugggghhhh!*" roared the ogre, jumping thirty feet into the air and landing with a *crunchhh!* that set the ground shaking.

Harry and Jill shook and shuddered even more, but at least the ogre didn't look so menacing now. In fact he seemed a bit frightened himself, for he said in a quiet voice, "What *was* that?"

Harry had realized by this time that the ogre was fascinated by the bubble. He started to explain about chewing bubble gum. In a minute or two he was persuading the ogre that chewing bubble gum might be more interesting than chewing *them*, and a couple of minutes after that saw the ogre reach out a huge hand to Jill, who began counting cubes of bright pink bubble gum into it.

"It's going to be much more fun than eating people," Harry assured him, "and what's more, it's good for the stomach."

That settled it. With a cautious and nervous grin, the ogre began chewing. His teeth clashed, and his smile widened. And when the first bubble emerged from his thick lips and went *plopp!* he laughed out loud.

"I can do it!" he roared.

"And we can go?" Jill said. "I've got a few more for you."

"More for me?" The ogre grinned. "How kind, O damsel. Now, watch this!"

They watched and admired him. And then while he was busy blowing ogre-sized bubbles, they murmured good-bye and went on their way along the grim and twisty path, which led, so Siggy said, to the Miserable Marsh.

"Just a moment!" called the ogre, sending shivers down their spines. But he only wanted them to see his latest bubble. "Byeeeeeee!" he called, and they breathed out loud and long.

"Phew," said Harry. "Well, that's the first task over. How about that, Siggy? We got past the ogre."

But the magic sword was sulking. "Bubble gum!" he snorted. "Who ever heard of an adventure with pink bubbles? It's against all tradition."

"But we did get past safely," said Jill. "That's the important thing."

"No, it's not the important thing," growled Siggy. "The important thing is having a terrible and unequal combat in which there is much chopping off of limbs and heads, and finally a disaster for one fighter or the other. Or both of them. And what did we get? Pink bubbles! You'll need more than that to get past the Bad Wizard, Harry. If you don't find the answer to his impossible riddle, then you'll both end up as toads, doomed to wander around the Miserable Marsh forever!"

He was sounding so gloomy as they came out of the Enchanted Forest and saw the Miserable Marsh that Harry had to tell him it wasn't as bad as it was made out to be, going on a desperate quest, and Jill was about to agree with him — when the Bad Wizard suddenly appeared in a flash of purple flame and a cloud of green and yellow smoke.

6

Whooshhh! Boom! Ffzzzzzz!

It was the Bad Wizard again, no doubt about it. There he was with his black wizard's hat and his *ho-ha-ho's*. Right away he promised he was going to change them into toads.

"Welcome, you two!" he jeered. "Soon you'll be croaking and crawling with all the other would-be rescuers. One redheaded toad and one skinny one if you don't guess the answer to my impossible riddle, and you won't. I'm going to enjoy this little contest of wits, ho-ho-ha-hee!"

Jill shook, and Harry shuddered, and even Siggy gave out a little moan, and the Bad Wizard looked even more pleased with himself.

"Think of something," Harry hissed to the magic sword, but Siggy muttered back that he was only good at chopping things up.

"How about bubble gum again?" whispered Jill. "I kept a couple for myself."

"I heard all that with my excellent hearing," the Bad Wizard told them. "And you won't fool me, the way you fooled the ogre. I'm not a dum-dum who falls for bubble gum! Heeee-heee-hee, toads, that's what you'll be! Listen, you can hear them croaking in the marsh. Listen to them!"

They listened. And they looked. There were hundreds of toads, each one of them either a prince or a knight or a hero. And they were all croaking that they didn't like it much in the mud and the rain, except for one small toad who was singing happily to himself.

"Maybe you'll think of the answer, Harry,"

said Siggy. "Not all the heroes get turned into toads."

"But I bet most of them do," Harry muttered gloomily.

"You're right, hee-hee-hee!" cackled the Bad Wizard. And he drew out of thin air a huge black book with a black iron key.

"Here we are," said the Bad Wizard when he had unlocked his Riddle Book. "You get only one guess, and if it isn't right, it's toad-time! Right, toads?"

A lot of croaks came from the toads, and to Jill they sounded just like toads, but to Harry the croaking noises began to make a pattern, and then they began to sound like words. Could it be that they were trying to tell him something? He didn't have time to figure it out, though, because the Bad Wizard was ready.

"Listen!" he snapped. "I'm only going to say it once! And you only get one guess, remember? Now:

Runs all day and never walks;
Often murmurs, never talks;
It has a bed and never sleeps;
It has a mouth and never eats.

"Well, what is it? Eh, little redheaded boy with two H's on your chest? I'll leave you for a few minutes, but I'll be back!" And with a *whoosh* and a *ffzzzz!* he vanished.

Harry watched the smoke drift away. "It's impossible! It's supposed to run and not sleep or something and eat without walking, or do I have that part wrong? Jill!"

"I don't know!" she said. "What was that part about murmuring? And not going to bed?"

"I've forgotten," moaned Harry. "Anyway, I'm no good at riddles. My brain hurts when we do ordinary work at school. We'll never guess the answer!"

"Siggy, you think of something!" cried Jill. "And scram, you horrible toads!" she yelled, as a couple of toads crawled around and twitched at the hem of her dress. "Go away!"

"Running and not eating?" Harry said. "What does that mean? I don't know! And shut up, you toads, I'm trying to think! What? What's that?"

"What's what?" said Jill. "Now what are you doing?"

Harry was bending down to listen to the toads, but why?

"Jill, they're talking to us," he whispered. "Listen, they're telling us something about the answers! What was that again?" he asked a couple of large toads. "Look at what?"

Half a dozen toads began to chorus.

"Look-at-the-answers-look-at-the-answers!"

"The answers?" said Jill, and suddenly she understood. "Yes! The Bad Wizard's left his Riddle Book open. Come on!"

They crept forward carefully, expecting at any moment to hear an evil cackling of glee, but nothing happened. They went right up to the huge book and looked at the yellow parchment.

But Harry groaned in disappointment, for the writing was unreadable.

It was a mass of strange and weird squiggles, like no writing he had ever seen before. It had to be secret and mysterious or probably magic writing, known only to wizards and suchlike. He let out another moan to Jill, who was looking at the writing and trying to read it, too, when the Bad Wizard once again appeared with his usual fireworks and pollution.

"No use, O skinny damsel!" He chuckled. "No one can read my magic writing except me, the very smart and terribly evil Bad Wizard! You've failed, haven't you?"

Harry agreed. But Jill hadn't given up. She had looked at the writing the right way up, then upside down, and she'd squinted at it out of the corners of her eyes, and then suddenly she'd realized that it wasn't as magic as it seemed, for she had put her mirror just *there*, and —

"Harry!" she hissed. "I've got the answer."

"Ready for toad-time?" cackled the Bad

Wizard, and he was so busy laughing he didn't hear Jill whispering to Harry. "Give up?" the wizard demanded.

"No," said Harry. "I've got the answer."

"Whattt!" the Bad Wizard screeched.

"You know, O Harry?" said Siggy, and when Harry said the answer was a river, Siggy boomed out Harry's praises all over the Miserable Marsh. "What a hero! Praise Harry, the conqueror of the Bad Wizard!"

"It was easy," said Harry. "I could have guessed it myself if I'd had more time." Jill didn't bother to argue with him as he went on: "I mean, what else runs along a bed down to a mouth but a river? I didn't need Jill to look in the mirror and — "

"A *mirror!*" screeched the Bad Wizard. "I've been tricked! My best riddle has been solved by this little hero's skinny damsel companion! That's cheating! It wasn't fair," he moaned, but Siggy said anything was fair against enchantment, so the Bad Wizard had to let them pass. "And I suppose that now you have defeated me I have to obey you in all things?" he grumbled to Harry and Jill.

They told him yes, so in a few moments all the toads had been turned back into handsome princes, knights, and ordinary heroes, all except for the little one who decided to stay a toad. He explained that he liked it in the Miserable Marsh, since he was fond of hopping about. "If you don't mind, I'll stay here with the Bad Wizard to keep him company," he told them, which made the Bad Wizard feel slightly better.

As the rest of the princes, knights, and heroes lined up to thank Harry and Jill before returning to their native countries, the Bad Wizard began to cackle once more.

"You might have fooled the ogre with bubbles, and you might have tricked me with your mirror, O skinny damsel, but you won't get your dozy doggy back again, oh, no! Wait till you see the dragon coming out of the sky with his fiery breath! You can invite me to the barbecue, hee-hee-heee. Oh, I like that: barbecued damsel, barbecued hero! What a witty Bad Wizard I am!"

Harry and Jill left him to his evil chuckling. They went on their way feeling excited and happy, in spite of their soggy shoes. But as they left the mists of the Miserable Marsh and saw the dragon's hollow mountain in the distance, Siggy said they'd better walk more quietly.

Squish-squish went their shoes. *Squish-squish-squish!*

"Quietly," advised Siggy.

"We can't," said Harry. Siggy said they'd better try, for the dragon could hear the lightest footfall on his hollow mountain, and instantly he would come roaring down, blasting out fire and smoke.

The children walked much more quietly after that, but it wasn't easy, not when your shoes were full of water, was it?

7

"Poor Queenie," whispered Jill, as they crept along. "I wonder how she's feeling."

"She won't be feeling anything except sleepy," Harry muttered. "You only have to look at Queenie to feel tired yourself. Hey, maybe she's made the dragon feel sleepy! Maybe he's asleep inside his mountain. We can creep up and grab Queenie while they're both snoring. Come on!"

Harry had convinced himself that the dragon *must* be asleep, otherwise why couldn't he hear them coming up his mountain, and Jill was trying to make herself believe it, when she happened to look up.

"Funny," she said. "There's a red shooting star up there, and it isn't dark yet."

Harry looked up, too. "It's moving fast."

"Moving here," groaned Jill. "And I don't think it's a shooting star."

"No, it's the dragon!" boomed Siggy. "Run!"

They heard the clashing of leathery wings and the clanging of scales, then the sudden rush of fire as the bushes and trees before them burst into flames, and another noise, one that a dragon shouldn't make. It sounded a little like barking.

"At least my shoes are drying out," puffed Jill as they ran. "I hate wet feet. Is it coming back?"

Harry stopped and looked up. "Yes, it is," he said, getting his breath back. "Siggy, I thought I heard barking. Do dragons ever bark?"

"Not usually," said the magic sword. "Not any I've ever seen. They roar and hiss."

"They usually do what this one's doing," said

Jill. "Burn things up. Here it comes again!"

They ran. And down zoomed the dragon, smoke belching from its nostrils. Down, down, it came, clanging its scales and beating its wings and jangling its spiked tail and barking furiously. . . .

"It *is* barking," said Harry. "Dragon!" he yelled. "That is you barking, isn't it?"

"I wish you'd stop annoying it," puffed Jill. "It can't be barking, look at it — hey, *look* at it, there's something on its back! Why it's — "

"Queenie!" cried Harry. "It's Queenie who's doing all the barking. Come here, Queenie!" he ordered, and to their surprise the dragon came closer until it was on the ground, with Queenie on its back.

It crept toward them and carelessly sent a burst of flame near Jill. She jumped out of the way, but not before her dress started smoking.

"I'm on fire!" she yelled. "Look at my lovely dress. It's all singed around the hem. Do something, Harry!"

Harry just stood there.

It was all happening a bit too quickly for him. First, the dragon had zoomed down — *barking*. Then it wasn't the dragon barking, it was Queenie.

But what was poor old Queenie doing up there on a fire-breathing dragon? And what was Jill yelling about?

"O Harry, this is your time to be a hero!" exclaimed Siggy.

And now Siggy was joining in, so what with Jill yelling, Queenie barking, the dragon starting little fires off among the bushes, and now this magic sword talking about being a hero. . . . Well, thought Harry, what am I supposed to *do?*

"Be heroic!" boomed Siggy.

"It's time he was!" declared Jill. "Who saved you from the ogre, Harry? With bubble gum? And who found the mirror writing to get the riddle right? Me, I did. Now it's your turn to do something!"

"But what!" said Harry.

Then someone else joined in.

Woooosh! Fizzz! Bangg!

"Oh, not you, too!" Harry groaned as the Bad Wizard appeared. "I expect you've got some advice to offer as well!"

The Bad Wizard was looking sneaky and pleased with himself. "I'm not here to offer advice," he said to Harry.

"Then why are you here?" Harry asked.

"Why? I'm here, my silly little hero in silver tights, to watch you try to fight the dragon to rescue that yappy spaniel of yours. Ho-ho-ha-ha-ho! I'm going to have a seat while I watch you get barbecued! *And* that sneaky and skinny damsel who thinks she's so smart!"

Jill glared at the Bad Wizard. Then she glared at Harry.

Harry knew that it was all up to him.

He gulped for a moment or two.

He looked up at Queenie on the dragon's back.

Then he crossed his fingers for luck and waved Siggy around his head.

"I'm coming for you, Queenie!" he yelled. "Harry the Hero will save you!"

Then he closed his eyes and charged.

"One barbecued hero coming up!" cackled the Bad Wizard. "Closely followed by roasted skinny damsel!"

On rushed Harry, still with his eyes closed.

"Harry, look out!" yelled Jill, but Harry wasn't going to open his eyes, not for anyone.

He could feel the air getting warmer, and he knew he was near the dragon, but he kept on. On and on, until he tripped over something, and in the shock of tumbling over, he opened his eyes and saw a huge knobbly green toe.

"Uh-ooohhh!" he cried, for he had banged the dragon's little toe.

"*BRAAUUUUGHGHGHGHHHHHHH!*" came a vast roar, louder than trains in tunnels, deeper than foghorns at sea, a real monster's roar.

And Harry saw the toe disappear as the dragon flapped its leathery wings and zoomed straight up into the sky.

"Very heroic!" boomed Siggy. "Prepare yourself for when the dragon comes down, O Harry!"

Then something started growling behind Harry, something noisy and angry. It was hanging on to his cloak, and it sounded very fierce.

"It's got me!" cried Harry. "Help, Jill!"

He tried to turn around, but he couldn't. And when he looked up, there was the dragon, hovering in the sky, with its wings slowly beating and little flames coming from its huge mouth.

"On with the barbecue!" shrieked the Bad Wizard.

Harry groaned. Once again, it was all too much for him.

But wait, something was wrong.

The dragon was up there — so what was doing the growling down *here*?

Then he looked behind him and saw what had hold of his cloak. It was Queenie!

"Curses!" howled the Bad Wizard. "Can't anything go right on Mandragora anymore?"

"This is most improper," Siggy scolded. "Harry, again, this is untraditional."

Harry gave up and sat down. Then the dragon flew over and sat down, too. Then, to Harry's surprise, Queenie woofed happily at the dragon and rubbed herself against its great knobbly green feet.

"I give up," he moaned. "I don't know what's going on anymore."

"I do," said Jill, and she was laughing at him, but not in a nasty sort of way, which was a change. "Harry, Queenie *likes* the dragon. See?"

It was true. Queenie was wagging her tail. And so was the dragon.

"It is so, O Harry," said Siggy reluctantly. "How this came to be, I cannot tell, but it seems that your faithful hound has tamed the dreadful dragon."

Harry perked up at that. "And I won't have to fight it or anything?"

"Unfortunately not," complained the Bad Wizard. "It seems that barbecued hero is not on the menu today. My plan has been ruined, and I have been beaten!"

Siggy cheered up, too, when he heard the Bad Wizard complaining.

"Yes," said Siggy. "The three tasks have now been accomplished. You have been outwitted by a damsel of superior intellect, O Bad Wizard. And Harry was in the end a most fitting hero. The faithful hound has been rescued, and the quest is now ended."

"And we've got to get back in time for supper," said Jill. "You know what your mom's like when you're late, Harry."

So Harry got to his feet and patted the dragon's huge green toe.

"I'm sorry I startled you, dragon," he said. "Say good-bye to Queenie. We're off now."

"Come on, Queenie," said Jill, but Queenie didn't. And she wouldn't.

Queenie backed away when Jill and Harry tried to get hold of her collar.

"Queenie, what's wrong?" said Harry.

"Oh, dear," said Jill, as Queenie scrambled up onto the dragon's back. "She likes it here on Mandragora."

"What?" cried Harry, as he began to understand. "Queenie, you can't stay here! We're going back to Belle Vue Mansions for supper."

But Queenie wouldn't come down. Jill was right. She wanted to stay with her new friend.

Harry looked at Jill, and she looked at Queenie. What were they to do? Jill could imagine what Harry's mom would say if they went back without the spaniel. It would be awful!

"Come on, it's time you thought of something, Siggy," said Harry, whirling the magic sword around his head. "So far you've managed to do nothing but chop a few twigs off a wicked tree. You complained about getting past the ogre with bubble gum, and you weren't much help with the Bad Wizard. What now, Siggy?"

The magic sword flashed rainbows all over the dragon's mountain. Then at last Siggy hollered that he'd thought of something. And if Harry would calm down and stop whirling him around, he'd tell them what it was.

"We'll ask the Bad Wizard," Siggy said. "He's tricky enough to work out what to do. And he still must obey you as long as we're on Mandragora. Ho there, Sneaky One!"

"Well?" grumbled the Bad Wizard. "What is it this time?"

When Harry and Jill explained that Queenie didn't want to leave Mandragora, the Bad Wizard muttered and complained for a while, but then at last he chuckled evilly.

"So your dragon-loving spaniel wants to stay here on Mandragora, does she? And your mom's going to be furious if Floppy-ears doesn't go home. Well, I'm bound to obey your wishes, since you won our contest, even if you did trick me. And it's an interesting little problem, which only I am clever enough to solve, me, the Bad

Wizard. Now, Queenie," he said, "can you remember a little spell? Lift those floppy ears of
yours, and listen!"

Queenie's floppy ears twitched.

Then the Bad Wizard pushed his tall black hat
to the back of his head and creaked down onto
his hands and knees. His nose was almost touch-
ing Queenie's soft muzzle.

"What's he *doing*?" demanded Jill, as the Bad
Wizard let out a string of woofs, growls, snorts,
squeaks, moans, and grunts.

Siggy explained that the Bad Wizard was
teaching Queenie a spell, and when Jill wanted
to know what sort of spell, the Bad Wizard
creaked to his feet in his usual bad-tempered
way.

"What sort of spell?" he said. "Why, a coming-
and-going spell, naturally. And before you ask
what *that* is, I'll tell you. This drippy dog of
yours now has the power to return to Mandragora whenever she wishes. Will that be all?"

He didn't wait for a reply.

Whizzz-flash-bangggg!

And that was the last they saw of the Bad Wizard.

Harry and Jill were dazzled once more, but Queenie had a knowing look in her soft brown eyes.

"The quest is ended!" boomed Siggy.

And so it was.

Into the blackness they hurtled, a bit tired and very hungry, but thrilled to bits, all of them.

8

Harry and Jill (and Queenie) were walking along the canal on their way back to Belle Vue Mansions when Freddie Peck from school came along on his bike.

They didn't see him, but he saw them.

"Who's *that?*" he said. "Why, it's Harry Taggart. Oh, oh, look at him! In silver tights, and Jill's in a nightgown!"

Harry looked down. Jill looked down.

"Siggy, we're not on Mandragora now!" yelled Jill. "Get us out of these clothes."

Freddie Peck hooted with laughter. "Wait till I tell the kids at school about you two. What are the two H's for, Harry? Helpless Harry?"

"Harry the Hero!" Jill called back angrily.

"Him!" hooted Freddie Peck. "Him, a hero? Oh-oh-oh!"

"Yes, O Stupid One!" boomed Siggy, and Freddie went quiet and absolutely still.

"Who said that?" he whispered. "It wasn't you two."

"I did," Siggy announced. "I, Sigismund, the Magic Sword, O Witless Child on the bike!" and Freddie fell off his bike, and then he fell over Harry, too.

Harry didn't know what was happening, and anyway he was too embarrassed to care. Freddie crashed into him, making him lose his balance, and it was only by good luck that Jill was able to grab the hem of his cloak and pull him back from the edge of the canal.

All was confusion and noise. Freddie Peck yelled as he hit the ground. Jill yelled as she pulled Harry back. Harry yelled as he saw the black water of the canal getting nearer. And Queenie barked wildly at them all.

Siggy joined in the noise, for it was time the magic ended.

"Farewell, O Harry! Farewell, O damsel!" he boomed, and Harry automatically waved Siggy around. And Harry found that for the first time since the adventure had begun he was able to release his grip on the magic sword.

Away went Siggy, far out over the black water of the canal.

"Bye! Bye, Siggy!" called the two children, while Freddie stood with his mouth wide open, making little choking noises.

The last echoes of Siggy's booming "Farewell!" had hardly stopped ringing in their ears when Harry and Jill realized that they were in their own clothes again, the same clothes in which they had left Belle Vue Mansions. Freddie Peck realized it, too.

"Hey, Harry Taggart and Jill Dakin," he said. "You were in some very funny clothes just a minute ago. And where'd that talking sword go? I want to know — "

But Harry and Jill had left. They weren't interested in what Freddie Peck wanted to know. They were late!

Harry's mom was at the door to meet them.

"You two certainly took your time," she said. "Hello, Queenie. Where have you been? Not telling, are you? You won't go running off again, will you?"

Queenie rolled on her back and let herself be petted, but there was a strange gleam in her eyes, which would have been recognized at once by anyone who knew about Mandragora.